Mrs. Lilly Is Silly!

Dan Gutman

Pictures by
Jim Paillot

HARPER
An Imprint of HarperCollinsPublishers

To Emma

Library of Congress Cataloging-in-Publication Data is available.
ISBN 978-0-06-196921-8 (lib. bdg.)—ISBN 978-0-06-196920-1 (pbk.)

Typography by Joel Tippie
14 15 CG/RRDH   10 9 8 7 6 5 4 3
❖
First Edition

Contents

1. Career Day   1

2. Mrs. Lilly Has to Go   10

3. How to Grab Somebody's Eyeballs   17

4. Digging Up Dirt   30

5. Ms. LaGrange Is Strange   37

6. The Truth About Mr. Docker   45

7. Andrea Goes Crazy   52

8. Front-Page News   63

9. The Scoop of the Century!   71

10. Stop the Presses!   78

11. Freedom of the Press   87

12. Lies! All Lies!   99

Career Day

My name is A.J. and I hate spiders. Aren't spiders gross? Yesterday I was in my backyard, and one of those disgusting things crawled up my leg. I thought I was gonna die!

Something else really weird happened yesterday. It was Friday. I walked into Mr.

Granite's class at school, and there were three grown-ups sitting on chairs in front of the whiteboard: a fireman, a cowboy, and a frogman.

"Who are *they*?" whispered my friend Ryan, who will eat anything, even stuff that isn't food.

"Those guys must have escaped from the loony bin," said Michael, who never ties his shoes.

We were all talking, until Mr. Granite held up his hand and made a peace sign, which means "shut up." Some other grown-ups came in and sat in front of the whiteboard.

"Good morning, everyone," said Mr.

Granite. "Dr. Carbles, the president of the Board of Education, decided that today would be Career Day at Ella Mentry School. So I invited a few of my friends to come in and tell you about their jobs. Maybe this will help you decide what *you* want to be when you grow up."

"I already know what *I'm* going to be," I said. "A pro skateboarder."

"Me too," said Alexia, who is a girl but is cool anyway.

"I want to be a veterinarian," said Andrea Young, this annoying girl with curly brown hair that I hate.

"You want to grow up and not eat meat?" I asked.

"That's a *vegetarian*, Arlo!" Andrea said, rolling her eyes. She calls me by my real name because she knows I don't like it. Why can't a truck full of vegetarians fall on Andrea's head?

The frogman stood up first. He had a mask on his face and flippers on his feet.

"I'm a scuba diver," he told us. "I feed the fish at the aquarium blah blah blah."

He told us all about how he feeds the fish. Then the cowboy stood up.

"I milk the cows and groom the horses and blah blah blah," he said. He told us what it was like to work on a ranch. Then some other guy stood up.

"I'm an exterminator," he said. "My job

is to kill bugs and blah blah blah."

Grown-ups sure have weird jobs!

"Our next guest is a special surprise," Mr. Granite told us. "Please welcome . . . professional skateboarder Tony Eagle!"

Wow! Tony Eagle is *famous*! He's been on TV. Me and the guys and Alexia started clapping and shouting.

Tony Eagle came rolling into the room. But he didn't come rolling in on a skateboard. He came rolling in on a wheelchair!

"What happened to *you*?" I asked.

"I broke every bone in my body," Tony told us.

"You must have been working on a really awesome new trick, huh?" asked

Neil, who we call the nude kid even though he wears clothes.

"No."

"Were you trying to jump over a car?" I asked. "That is cool!"

"No."

"What happened?" asked Ryan.

"I . . . uh . . . ran into a door," said Tony Eagle.

Ouch! Running into doors hurts. Maybe I don't want to be a pro skateboarder after all.

A bunch of other grown-ups told us about their jobs. A lawyer told us that he argues with people all day. A nurse told us that she has to clean up blood and guts and puke at a hospital. The fireman told us that one time a burning building collapsed while he was in it.

And I thought going to *school* was no fun! After Career Day, I'm not sure I want to grow up to be a grown-up at *all*. I think I'll just stay a kid for the rest of my life.

When they were all done, the grown-ups started to leave. But you'll never believe who ran into the door at that moment.

Nobody! If you ran into a door, you could end up in a wheelchair like Tony Eagle.

But you'll never believe who ran into the *doorway*.

I'm not gonna tell you.

Okay, okay, I'll tell you! But you have to read the next chapter. So nah-nah-nah boo-boo on you!

Mrs. Lilly Has to Go

It was a lady who came running into our classroom. She was wearing an old-time man's hat and a trench coat.* There was a camera around her neck and a notepad in her hand. She was all out of breath.

*I guess a trench coat is a coat that you wear in a trench.

"Is Career Day over?" she asked.

"Mrs. Lilly!" said Mr. Granite.

I recognized Mrs. Lilly. She's a reporter for our local paper, the *News Tribune Bulletin Inquirer.* She wrote an article about our school when a squirrel ate through the power lines and all the lights went out. They put my picture in the paper and everything. My mom put it up on the refrigerator.

"Sorry I'm late," Mrs. Lilly said. "I had to

write a big story about a tree."

"Why did you write about a tree?" asked Andrea.

"Yeah, why did you write about a tree?" asked Emily, who always does whatever Andrea does.

"It fell down," said Mrs. Lilly.

"So what?" asked Ryan. "Don't trees fall down all the time?"

"Well, this tree landed on a house."

"Was anybody hurt?" asked Emily, all worried.

"No."

"Then why was it a big story?" asked Mr. Granite.

"The tree fell on Mayor Hubble's house,"

Mrs. Lilly told us.

"Oh, and that's a big story?" asked Alexia.

"Well, it landed on the mayor's bathroom," Mrs. Lilly said, "and the mayor was *in* the bathroom at the time. You see, a tree falling down is boring. And a tree falling down on the mayor's house is still pretty boring. But a tree falling down on the mayor's bathroom while he's on the toilet is a great human interest story. That's what I look for: human interest stories."

"What happened to Mayor Hubble?" asked Emily, all concerned.

"He had to go," said Mrs. Lilly.

"Of course he had to go," I said. "That's why he was in the bathroom."

"No," said Mrs. Lilly. "I mean, after he went, he had to go."

"How can you go right after you went?" asked Neil the nude kid.

We went back and forth like that for a while until Mr. Granite interrupted.

"I'm terribly sorry," he said. "This is all very interesting, but we have to do our math lesson now."

Ugh. I hate math.

"That's too bad," said Mrs. Lilly. "I wanted to show the kids how we make the newspaper."

"Oh, that would be neat!" said Andrea.

"Don't you want to learn how they make the newspaper?"

"Yes!" said all the girls except for Alexia.

"No!" said all the boys and Alexia.

"Maybe you can come back another time to show the class how to make a newspaper," suggested Mr. Granite.

"I have a better idea," said Mrs. Lilly. "When I come back, the kids and I can make a real newspaper *together*!"

"That's a *wonderful* idea!" said Mr. Granite. "Would you kids like to make a real newspaper with Mrs. Lilly?"

"Yes!" yelled all the girls except for Alexia.

"No!" yelled all the boys and Alexia.

"I can see the headline now," said Mrs. Lilly. "'KIDS MAKE NEWSPAPER!' I love it! But for now, I've got to go."

"Do you have to go, or do you have to *go*?" I asked.

"I have to go," she replied, "and it's an emergency!"

I still didn't know if Mrs. Lilly had to go, or if she had to *go*. In any case, she went running out of the room.

Mrs. Lilly is silly.

How to Grab Somebody's Eyeballs

"Okay," Mr. Granite said after Mrs. Lilly was gone, "turn to page twenty-three in your math books."

We all took out our math books and turned to page twenty-three. But you'll never believe who walked into the

doorway a few minutes later.

It was Mrs. Lilly again!

"Mrs. Lilly! I thought you said you had to go," said Mr. Granite. "To what do we owe the pleasure of your company *now*?"

(That's grown-up talk for "What are *you*

doing here?")

"I did have to go," Mrs. Lilly replied. "And I went. Now I'm back."

"I'm glad a tree didn't fall on you," I told her.

"But I thought you were going to come back another *day*," said Mr. Granite. "We're starting our math lesson now."

"Math, eh?" Mrs. Lilly said. "Well, if we print up a newspaper with ten pages in it and there are five articles on each page, how many articles can we fit into the newspaper?"

Some kids raised their hands. Mrs. Lilly called on Little Miss I-Know-Everything, of course.

"Fifty!" said Andrea. "Because five tens make fifty."

"Correct!" said Mrs. Lilly. "See, we just did a math lesson. Now let's write some of those articles for our newspaper."

"Yay!" we all shouted.

"I give up," said Mr. Granite. "If you need me, I'll be in the teachers' lounge."

He went to the teachers' lounge, which is a secret room where the teachers go to have hot tub parties.

Mrs. Lilly took off her trench coat, and we all gathered around her on the floor.

"What should we write about?" asked Emily.

"Write about what you know," said Mrs.

Lilly. "You know a lot about your school. How about we make a school newspaper? We can call it . . . *The Ella Mentry Sentry.* You can all write articles for it."

"Yay!" everybody yelled.

Little Miss Annoying was all excited, and she was waving her hand around like it was on fire.

"I already wrote something at home," Andrea announced, pulling some papers out of her desk. "Maybe we can use it in our newspaper."

Ugh. Could she possibly be more boring? Only Andrea would write an article for a newspaper before she even knew we were going to *make* a newspaper. She held up her dumb article so we could all see it. The first page said:

I LOVE ELLA MENTRY SCHOOL

By Brenda Myers

"Who's Brenda Myers?" asked Alexia.

"That's my pen name," said Andrea.

"You name your pens?" I said. "That's weird."

Andrea rolled her eyes and then she read her article out loud. It was all about how our school was built in 1961, and it was named after a teacher named Ella Mentry. Then it went on to talk about a bunch of other really boring stuff, like the history of the school. I thought I was gonna die from boredom.

When the torture was over, Andrea looked up at Mrs. Lilly and waited for her to say how wonderful that dumb article was. What a brownnoser! But that's when the most amazing thing in the history of the world happened.

Mrs. Lilly dropped Andrea's article into the garbage can!

"That was terrible," she said.

"Oh, snap!" said Ryan.

Well, Andrea looked like she was going to *explode*! I don't think a grown-up *ever* said anything like *that* to her. Ha-ha! Nah-nah-nah boo-boo on Andrea! In her face!

It was the greatest moment of my life.

"*The Ella Mentry Sentry* needs to reach out and grab the reader's eyeballs," Mrs. Lilly told us.

"Ouch!" I said. "I don't want anybody touching my eyeballs."

"What I mean is that newspapers have to compete with the internet, TV, and video games," Mrs. Lilly told us. "Our paper needs to have *exciting* stories."

"I thought your article was wonderful, Andrea," whispered Emily, who loves everything Andrea does.

"But our school is really boring," said Michael. "I don't think we can make an exciting newspaper that will grab people's eyeballs."

"Nothing interesting ever happens here," said Ryan.

"Yeah," said Neil the nude kid, "this school is boring. We don't have any good stories to tell."

"Sure you do!" Mrs. Lilly said. "You've just got to dig for them."

At that moment Mr. Klutz came into the classroom. He's our principal, and he has no hair at all. I mean none. His head looks like a lightbulb.*

"We're making a newspaper all about the school," said Mrs. Lilly. "Can we

---

*Not one of those curly lightbulbs. That would be weird.

interview you, Mr. Klutz?"

"Certainly!" he replied. "A school news-paper is a great idea. What would you like to know about me?"

I thought Mrs. Lilly was going to ask

Mr. Klutz what it was like to be a principal and boring stuff like that. But she didn't.

"Tell us, Mr. Klutz," said Mrs. Lilly, "when did you lose your hair?"

Everybody gasped. Nobody had ever asked Mr. Klutz about his hair before.

"That's personal!" said Andrea. "We shouldn't ask people questions like that."

"Oh, I don't mind," Mr. Klutz said. "Let's see.... I remember my wedding pictures. I had a full head of hair when I first got married. My hair started falling out around the time my wife and I got divorced. And by the time I got married again, I was totally bald."

Mr. Klutz told us some more stuff about

the good old days when he had hair and then he said he had to go.

"Do you have to go," I asked, "or do you have to *go*?"

"I have to go," he said.

Mr. Klutz left, and Mrs. Lilly went over to the whiteboard.

"So we're going to write an article about Mr. Klutz's hair?" asked Alexia.

"No, I have another idea," said Mrs. Lilly. "Let me show you how I would handle this interview. It's a great human interest story. I can see the headline now. . . ."

And then she wrote this on the whiteboard, with big letters . . .

MR. KLUTZ HAS TWO WIVES!

Digging Up Dirt

4

"Mr. Klutz has two wives?" asked Ryan.

"Sure!" Mrs. Lilly said. "He had one wife and then he got divorced and married somebody else. That's two wives."

"But he didn't have two wives at the

same time," Andrea pointed out.

"I never said he did," said Mrs. Lilly. "Now, what about the *other* grown-ups at Ella Mentry School? We need to dig up some dirt."

"You should go out to the playground," I suggested. "There's plenty of dirt there."

"Not *that* kind of dirt!" said Mrs. Lilly. "We need some hot stories that will grab people's eyeballs. Alexia and Emily, I want you to work as a team. Go sneak into the teachers' lounge. See what *really* goes on in there."

"Right, Chief!" said Emily.

"Ryan and Michael, you're a team, too," said Mrs. Lilly. "Go through all the garbage cans in the school. Find out if any teachers throw away anything interesting."

"We're on it!" said Michael.

"Neil," said Mrs. Lilly. "I want you to put a tail on Mr. Macky, the reading specialist."

"Why?" asked Neil. "People don't have tails."

"Not *that* kind of a tail!" Mrs. Lilly said. "I want you to follow Mr. Macky around. See where he goes. See who he talks to. Then report back to us."

"Got it, Chief!" said Neil.

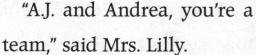

"A.J. and Andrea, you're a team," said Mrs. Lilly.

"*Oooooh!*" Ryan said. "A.J. and Andrea are a team. They must be in *love!*"

"When are you gonna get married?" asked Michael.

If those guys weren't my best friends, I would hate them.

"I want you to interview as many teachers as you can," Mrs. Lilly told Andrea and me. "Bring back some scoops."

"Why do you need scoops?" I asked. "Did your dog go to the bathroom?"

"Not *those* kind of scoops!" Mrs. Lilly shouted.

"Scoops are stories, Arlo," Andrea said, rolling her eyes.

"I knew that," I lied.

"Dig up some secrets," said Mrs. Lilly. "Get some information nobody else knows. You all have one hour. After that, report back here, and we'll put *The Ella Mentry Sentry* together on the computer. I can't wait to see how you make out."

"Ewwwwwwwww, disgusting!" we all shouted. "Mrs. Lilly said 'make out'!"

"What if we don't find any secrets?" Michael asked.

"Everybody has secrets," Mrs. Lilly said. "Go out there and find them. Ask the teachers to tell you something about themselves that nobody knows. And make sure to get your facts right. That's very important."

"But—"

"No buts! Go! Go! Go!"

We all giggled because Mrs. Lilly said "but," which sounds just like "butt" except that it only has one *t.* But "butt" is a lot funnier than "but." Nobody knows why.

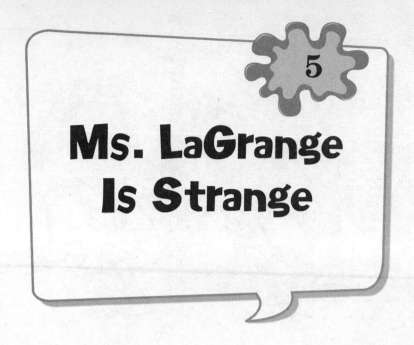

Ms. LaGrange
Is Strange

Andrea grabbed her notebook and a pencil. Then we went slinking down the hallway like secret agents. It was cool.

"Isn't this exciting, Arlo?" said Andrea. "We're like real investigative reporters. I hope we get some good interviews!"

"I have an idea," I said. "We should sneak out of school and go home. Then I could play video games for the rest of the day. Nobody would ever know we were gone."

"Shhhhhhhh!" Andrea said. "I think I hear somebody. Hold my hand."

"I'm not holding hands with you," I told her. "Reporters don't hold hands."

"They do if they're in *love*," she replied.

Ugh, disgusting! I thought I was gonna throw up.

We snuck around the corner, where I spotted an open door.

"The vomitorium!" we both said.

The vomitorium is where we eat lunch. It used to be called the cafetorium, but then one day some kid threw up in there, and it's been the vomitorium ever since.

The only person in the vomitorium was our lunch lady, Ms. LaGrange. She's from France, which is this country where they eat frogs' legs.

"Bonjour!" said Ms. LaGrange. (That's France talk for "hello.") "Lunch will not be ready for an hour. What can I do for you kids?"

Andrea got her pad and pencil ready so she could take notes.

"We're here to dig up some dirt," I told Ms. LaGrange.

"Well," she said, "there's dirt in the flowerpot on the windowsill."

"Not *that* kind of dirt!" Andrea told her. "We need a scoop."

Ms. LaGrange picked a scoop out of the sink.

"Here," she said, "you can use this scoop to dig up some dirt from the flowerpot."

"Not *that* kind of scoop!" said Andrea.

"We're making a school newspaper, so we need to interview you," I told Ms. LaGrange. "Tell us something about yourself that nobody knows."

"Hmmmm," Ms. LaGrange said.* "When

_____

*Grown-ups always say "Hmmmm" when they're thinking. Nobody knows why.

41

I was a little girl growing up in France, my parents owned a restaurant. . . ."

Ms. LaGrange started telling us all about her parents' restaurant. It sounded like it was going to be boring. But Little Miss Perfect was writing down every word in her notebook anyway.

"Um-hmm," Andrea said. "Go on."

"Well, one day," Ms. LaGrange said, "I was in the restaurant eating my lunch. It was soup. A nice tomato soup with little crackers blah blah blah . . ."

Ugh. I thought I was gonna die. Who cared what kind of soup it was? This was the most boring story in the history of the world. We were wasting our time interviewing Ms. LaGrange.

"So I was drinking my soup," she continued, "when I saw the reflection of a man's face in the soup bowl."

"So?" I asked, bored.

"And do you know whose reflection I saw in the soup?" she asked.

"Who?" asked Andrea.

"Elvis Presley!" Ms. LaGrange said. "He walked right into our restaurant and ate lunch there!"

"WOW," we said, which is "MOM" upside down.

"Now *that's* a scoop!" Andrea said. "Let's go tell Mrs. Lilly!"

We ran all the way back to our classroom. Mrs. Lilly was sitting at the computer. She had already typed THE ELLA MENTRY SENTRY on the screen, and below it were blank spaces where the articles would go. We told her about our interview with Ms. LaGrange.

"That's great!" she said. "This could be our lead story!"

Then she typed this out in big letters:

**LUNCH LADY SEES
GHOST OF ELVIS
IN SOUP BOWL!**

The Truth About Mr. Docker

Mrs. Lilly was really proud of us for the scoop we got from Ms. LaGrange.

"Great work, you two!" she said. "Now go out there and get us another story like that."

"Will do, Chief!" Andrea said.

We slinked down the hall like secret agents again. After a few minutes we got tired of slinking, but we bumped into Mr. Docker, our science teacher. He was coming out of the bathroom.

"We're doing interviews for the school paper," Andrea said. "Can you tell us something about yourself that nobody knows?"

"Hmmmm," said Mr. Docker, "let me think."

"Like maybe you have two wives," I suggested, "or you saw Elvis in a soup bowl."

"No, nothing like that," Mr. Docker said. "I guess I lead a pretty dull life. It's just work, work, work all the time."

It didn't seem like we were getting any-
where with Mr. Docker. He was boring.

"What do you do when you're not working?" asked Andrea.

"Oh, my wife and I like to exercise
together," he told us. "We go running every
Saturday. I even won a race last week."

"Really?" Andrea said, writing it all down in her pad. "That's exciting!"

"Did your wife run in the race too?" I asked.

"Oh yes," said Mr. Docker. "She did very well. She came in third place."

"We need to make sure we have all the facts right," I said. "So you ran in a race over the weekend. You came in first, and your wife came in third. Is that right?"

"Yes," said Mr. Docker. "We even got free T-shirts."

"Great!" I said. "Thanks for giving us an interview!"

Mr. Docker went to the science room. Andrea and I rushed back to our classroom.

"Isn't it exciting that Mr. Docker won a race over the weekend, Arlo?" Andrea said. "This is going to make a great article for the paper!"

"No it won't," I said. "That story is boring. I have a better story to write."

When we got to our classroom, Mrs. Lilly was at the computer working on *The Ella Mentry Sentry*. I told her we had another big scoop, and she said it would be okay if I typed the headline on the computer by myself. So I typed this:

MR. DOCKER BEATS HIS WIFE!

"You can't write that, Arlo!" Andrea said. "What a horrible thing to say! Mr.

Docker doesn't beat his wife!"

"He does too!" I said. "They were in a race. He won, and she came in third place. So he beat her. It's right there in your notes."

"Mrs. Lilly?" asked Andrea. "What do *you* say?"

Andrea looked at Mrs. Lilly. Mrs. Lilly looked at me. I looked at Mrs. Lilly. Mrs. Lilly looked at Andrea. We were all looking at each other. You could have heard a pin drop, if any of us had been holding pins. But why would anybody bring pins to school? That would be weird.

"This is front-page news!" Mrs. Lilly finally said. "Great job, A.J.! You are a natural reporter."

"Thank you!" I said.

I looked at Andrea and stuck my tongue out.

Andrea Goes Crazy

When Mrs. Lilly told me I was a natural reporter, Andrea's face got all red. I don't think a grown-up ever said that another kid was better than her at *anything*. It looked like Andrea wanted to yell and scream at Mrs. Lilly. But of course Little

Miss Brownnoser would never say any-thing mean to a grown-up, so Andrea just stood there with her eyes bugging out. I thought she was going to explode! It was the greatest moment of my life.

"Now go out there and dig up some more dirt," Mrs. Lilly told us. "We only have half an hour left."

Andrea and I went out into the hallway again. She was all mad, stomping around and making her best mean face at me.

"Anything you can do, I can do better, Arlo!" she said. "I'll show *you* who's a nat-ural reporter!"

"Sheesh," I said, "take a chill pill."

We wandered around the hallways for

a while until we saw Mrs. Yonkers in the computer room. She was by herself, so it must have been her free period.

Andrea marched over to Mrs. Yonkers and asked her to tell us the most exciting thing that ever happened to her.

"Oh, I'm not a very exciting person, I'm sorry to say," said Mrs. Yonkers. "I take my son to swimming practice, I go grocery shopping, and on the weekend we have barbecues in the backyard. . . ."

"You say you have barbecues in your backyard?" asked Andrea, writing down every word.

"Sure, almost every week," said Mrs. Yonkers. "It's fun."

"Great!" Andrea said. "Let's go, Arlo."

Having a barbecue in the backyard didn't sound like much of a scoop to me. But when we went out into the hallway, Andrea wrote this in her notebook:

**MRS. YONKERS
SETS FIRES FOR FUN!**

"She doesn't set fires for fun," I told Andrea.

"That's what she said!" Andrea insisted. "I have it right here in my notes! You're not the *only* natural reporter around here, Arlo. I can dig up the dirt, too. This is a great human interest story."

"Whatever," I said.

We saw our vice principal, Mrs. Jafee,

coming down the hall, and Andrea ran over to her.

"We're writing articles for the paper," she said. "Mrs. Jafee, what's the worst thing that ever happened to you?"

"Hmmm," said Mrs. Jafee. "I had a sad childhood. My family was very poor. There were even rats in our house. It was so bad, we had to use poison to get rid of them."

"Great!" said Andrea, writing in her notebook. When Mrs. Jafee left, I looked at what Andrea had written:

VICE PRINCIPAL LIVED WITH RATS!

But then Andrea crossed that out with her pencil.

"I have a better idea," she said. And then

she wrote this:

VICE PRINCIPAL POISONED
DEFENSELESS ANIMALS!

Andrea had this wild look in her eyes like crazy people do in the movies. It was scary! That's when the school security guard, Officer Spence, came over.

"Are you kids supposed to be roaming around in the halls?" he asked us.

"Sure," I told him. "We're writing articles for the school paper."

"Yes," Andrea said. "Security guards must lead very dangerous lives. Can you tell us about a time you beat up a bad guy, or something exciting like that?"

"No, I never beat up any bad guys," said Officer Spence. "But before I got this job,

I was a security guard in a prison. That wasn't much fun."

"How long did you work in the prison?" I asked.

"Oh, about five years."

Andrea got that crazy look in her eyes again while she was writing notes. It was almost like the time I hypnotized her and she climbed up on the roof. When Officer Spence walked away, she showed me what she had written in her notebook:

**OFFICER SPENCE WAS
IN JAIL FOR FIVE YEARS!**

"He was not!" I told Andrea.

"He was too!" she insisted. "I have it right here in my notes!"

We went back and forth like that for a while. Andrea was getting out of control!

After that she marched up to interview Ms. Coco, our gifted and talented teacher.

Ms. Coco told us that her car broke down the other day, and she had to use somebody else's car to drive to school. So Andrea wrote this in her notebook:

MS. COCO IS A CAR THIEF!

Then we went over to the office to interview Mrs. Patty, the school secretary. She told us a really sad story about the time her dog died in an accident when she was a little kid. But this is what Andrea wrote in her notebook:

MRS. PATTY—DOG KILLER!

I slapped my head. I was a little worried about all the dirt Andrea was digging up.

"I'm not sure we should put those articles in the paper," I told her as we walked back to our class. "We might get into big trouble."

"Oh, take a chill pill, Arlo," Andrea said. "Mrs. Lilly told us to dig up some dirt. I'm just doing what she told us to do."

Andrea *always* does what grown-ups tell her to do. A grown-up could tell her to go jump off a bridge, and Andrea would do it. What is her problem?

"We should probably interview Mr. Granite," I suggested. "After all, he is our teacher."

"We don't need to interview Mr. Granite,"

Andrea said. "I know exactly what to write about him."

She wrote this in her notebook:

**THIRD-GRADE TEACHER
IS AN ILLEGAL ALIEN!**

Well, at least that one was true. Mr. Granite *is* from another planet.

Front-Page News

Andrea and I did a bunch of interviews with the grown-ups at our school. When we got back to the classroom, Ryan was the only other kid who was there. He said that he and Michael didn't find anything interesting when they were going through the garbage can, so they decided to split up and work separately.

Andrea was all proud of herself for digging up dirt, and she showed Mrs. Lilly her notebook:

MRS. YONKERS SETS FIRES FOR FUN!

**VICE PRINCIPAL POISONED
DEFENSELESS ANIMALS!**

**OFFICER SPENCE WAS
IN JAIL FOR FIVE YEARS!**

MS. COCO IS A CAR THIEF!

MRS. PATTY—DOG KILLER!

**THIRD-GRADE TEACHER
IS AN ILLEGAL ALIEN!**

"These are terrific stories, Andrea!" Mrs. Lilly told her. "You and A.J. make a great team!"

"*Oooooh!*" Ryan said. "A.J. and Andrea make a great team. They must be in *love!*"

Andrea said she took a typing class after school (of course), so she was allowed to type her stories into the computer. She had that crazy look in her eyes the whole time.

Everybody else started filing back into class.*

"Did you dig up any good dirt?" Mrs. Lilly asked everyone. This one kid came in with a bucket full of dirt. *Real* dirt.

"Not *that* kind of dirt!" we all yelled at him.

What a dumbhead.

---

*They didn't actually come into class holding files. My dad has a file in his workshop down the basement. It would be weird to file in class.

Neil the nude kid came running into the classroom. He looked all excited.

"Did you dig up any dirt?" Mrs. Lilly asked him.

"I put a tail on Mr. Macky like you told me to," Neil said. "I followed him around for an hour, and guess what I caught him doing?"

"What?" we all asked.

"I saw Mr. Macky and Mrs. Daisy together," Neil said. "They were standing near the water fountain. And they were . . . *kissing*!"

Everybody gasped.

"Ewwww, disgusting!" me and the guys and Alexia went.

"Wait a minute," said Emily. "Mr. Macky and Mrs. Daisy are *married*."

"Ewwww!" I said. "That's even *more* disgusting."

"No, it's a great story!" Andrea said. Then she typed this into the computer:

MR. MACKY SPOTTED KISSING MARRIED WOMAN!

"I love it!" said Mrs. Lilly. "Put that on the front page! What else have you kids got?"

"Emily and I snuck into the teachers' lounge," said Alexia.

"What did you find in there?" asked Mrs. Lilly. "Any good dirt?"

"Did you see the hot tub?" I asked.

"No, nothing very exciting," Emily said. "There were just a bunch of teachers eating lunch."

"That's all?" asked Mrs. Lilly. "That's not a story."

"Yeah, it was really boring," Alexia said. "The most exciting thing that happened was that Miss Laney spilled some apple juice and had to clean it up."

Andrea suddenly looked up from the computer screen with those crazy eyes of hers. "What?" she asked. "Did you say Miss Laney spilled juice? That's a great human interest story!"

Then she typed this into the computer:

**SPEECH TEACHER HAS
A DRINKING PROBLEM**

"That's *genius*!" said Mrs. Lilly. "You are

a *great* reporter, Andrea!"

"Thank you!"

Andrea had a big, crazy-eyed smile on

her face, like she just won the No Bell Prize or something.* She just *loves* it when grown-ups tell her how wonderful she is.

"Hey," Neil the nude kid suddenly said, "where's Michael?"

We all looked around. Everybody was back in the classroom except for Michael.

"Yes, where *is* Michael?" asked Mrs. Lilly.

"The last time I saw him," Ryan said, "he was climbing into the Dumpster in the playground. He said he was looking for a scoop."

---

*That's a prize they give out to people who don't have bells.

The Scoop of the Century!

We didn't wait around for Michael to come back to class. We had a newspaper to finish.

Andrea typed her stories into the computer. Mrs. Lilly used a laptop computer to look up photos we could use. She found a picture of Elvis Presley and made it look like he was standing next to Ms. LaGrange. Then she found a picture of Officer Spence and drew bars in front of his face to make it look like he was in jail. She cut out a picture of Mrs. Yonkers smiling and put it in front of a picture of a house that was burning down.

Mrs. Lilly showed us how to put the photos into our classroom computer, and Andrea wrote captions under them:

Ms. LaGrange had an Elvis sighting while sipping soup.

Officer Spence behind bars.

When she's not teaching, Mrs. Yonkers enjoys setting fires.

The front page of *The Ella Mentry Sentry* looked great.

"I say this paper is done," said Mrs. Lilly. "Let's print it!"

Andrea hit the PRINT button, and the printer started printing. Because that's what printers do. But you'll never believe who ran into the door at that moment!

Nobody. Why would anyone run into a door? That would hurt. But you'll never believe who ran into the *doorway*.

It was Michael! He was wearing his backpack, and he was all out of breath.

"Did you get a scoop?" Mrs. Lilly asked him.

"I got the best scoop in the history of the world!" Michael replied.

"STOP THE PRESSES!" shouted Mrs. Lilly. "Michael has a scoop!"

Andrea stopped the printer. We all looked at Michael.

Now, I know what you're thinking. You're thinking the same thing I was thinking. You're thinking that Michael pulled a plastic scoop out of his backpack. You're thinking that we all yelled at him, "Not *that* kind of scoop!"

But Michael *didn't* pull a scoop out of his backpack. So nah-nah-nah boo-boo on you.

"What did you find out, Michael?" asked Mrs. Lilly.

"Mr. Klutz . . . doesn't wear underpants!" shouted Michael.

Everybody gasped! We were all freaking out!

"No!" shouted Alexia.

"It can't be true!" shouted Neil the nude kid.

"This is the scoop of the century!" shouted Andrea.

"Wait a minute," said Mrs. Lilly. "Calm down, everyone. We have to make sure we have our facts straight. Michael, do you have any proof that Mr. Klutz doesn't wear underpants?"

"Uh, not exactly," Michael said. "But I don't have any proof that he *does* wear underpants either. So I figure there's a fifty-fifty chance that Mr. Klutz doesn't wear underpants."

We all looked at Mrs. Lilly. She was a grown-up, so the decision would be up to her.

"Hmmm," she said. "Fifty-fifty, eh? Well, that's good enough for me. Andrea, put that on page two!"

Andrea typed this into the computer:

MR. KLUTZ DOESN'T
WEAR UNDERPANTS!

Stop the Presses!

Finally, *The Ella Mentry Sentry* was finished, and we were ready to print it. Mrs. Lilly told us we had all done a great job.

"Can I print out some extra copies so we can take the newspaper home and show it to our parents?" asked Andrea.

"Of course!" said Mrs. Lilly. "We'll print a copy for everyone in the class."

Andrea hit the PRINT button again, and the printer started printing a bunch of copies of *The Ella Mentry Sentry*. But you'll never believe in a million hundred years who came walking into the door at that moment.

Nobody. It would hurt if you walked into a door. I thought you would know that by now. But you'll never believe who poked his head in the door.

Nobody! Why would anyone in their right mind want to poke their head in a door? That would hurt too.

But you'll never believe who came

walking into our classroom.

It was Mr. Klutz!

"I just wanted to see how you kids were making out," he said.

"Ewwwwwwww, disgusting!" we all shouted. "We're not making out."

"No, I mean, how is your newspaper going?" asked Mr. Klutz.

"See for yourself," Mrs. Lilly said as she took a copy out of the printer and handed it to Mr. Klutz.

As he read the front page of our paper, his eyes bugged out and his jaw dropped open. He was white as a ghost!

"Are you okay, Mr. Klutz?" I asked him.

"STOP THE PRESSES!" he yelled.

"Officer Spence was in jail? Mrs. Yonkers sets buildings on fire? Mr. Docker beats his wife? Mrs. Patty kills dogs? You can't print this stuff!"

"Why not?" asked Mrs. Lilly. "Those are

great human interest stories."

"They're a bunch of lies!" Mr. Klutz said. He was really mad.

"Are you calling us liars?" asked Mrs. Lilly.

"If the shoe fits, wear it!" said Mr. Klutz.

"What do shoes have to do with anything?" I asked, but everybody ignored me.

"Where did you get this information?" demanded Mr. Klutz.

"I'm sorry," Mrs. Lilly told him, "but we cannot reveal our sources."

Mr. Klutz turned to page two of our paper and let out a scream. I guess he must have read the story about himself.

He was freaking out.

"I don't wear underpants?" Mr. Klutz yelled.

Everybody started giggling because Mr. Klutz just admitted out loud that he didn't wear underpants.

"How could you possibly know what I wear or don't wear under my clothes?" Mr. Klutz demanded.

"We only print the facts," said Mrs. Lilly. "We had no proof that you wear underpants, so we had no choice but to assume you don't."

"That's ridiculous!" shouted Mr. Klutz. "I most certainly *do* wear underpants, and I can prove it."

With that, Mr. Klutz pulled down his pants.

"EEEEEK!" Mrs. Lilly screamed. "Children! Don't look!"

But we all looked anyway. Under his pants, Mr. Klutz was wearing pink boxer shorts with red hearts on them. It was hilarious. You should have been there.

"Your underpants are adorable, Mr. Klutz," said Alexia.

It was a real Kodak moment. So Andrea quickly picked up Mrs. Lilly's camera and snapped a picture of Mr. Klutz with his pants down.

"We can use this in the *next* edition of *The Ella Mentry Sentry*!" Andrea said.

"There will *be* no next edition of *The Ella Mentry Sentry*!" Mr. Klutz shouted. "This newspaper is—"

But he didn't get the chance to finish his sentence, because you'll never believe

in a million hundred years who came running into the classroom at that moment.

I'm not going to tell you.

Okay, okay, I'll tell you.

But you have to read the next chapter
first. So nah-nah-nah boo-boo on you.

Freedom of the Press

The person who came running into the classroom at that moment was Dr. Carbles, the president of the Board of Education! He was the one who came up with the idea of Career Day in the first place.

"Klutz!" he shouted. "Why are you

standing there with your pants down?"

"I . . . I . . . I was just proving to the children that I wear underpants," Mr. Klutz explained.

"The children are here to learn about reading, writing, and arithmetic," yelled

Dr. Carbles. "They're not here to learn about your underwear."

"But . . . but . . . but . . ."

We all started giggling because Mr. Klutz kept saying "but," which sounds just like "butt"; but you can't say "butt" in school. Nobody knows why.

"Parading around in your underpants is not part of your job description, Klutz!" said Dr. Carbles. "You're fired!"

Everybody gasped. That's when a bunch of the teachers came running into the room.

"We heard that the students are writing mean stories about us in the school paper," shouted Mr. Macky. "Is this true?"

"Yes, it's true!" Mr. Klutz said, waving around a copy of *The Ella Mentry Sentry*. "Look at this! 'Mrs. Patty—Dog Killer!' 'Vice Principal Poisoned Defenseless Animals!'"

"You can't print that garbage!" shouted Ms. Coco.

"Sure we can," said Mrs. Lilly. "Didn't

you ever hear of freedom of the press? It's in the First Amendment."

"Well, I'm the president of the Board of Education," said Dr. Carbles as he grabbed all the papers out of the printer, "and what I say goes. I'm shutting down *The Ella Mentry Sentry* right now!"

Everybody gasped.

"That's not fair!" Ryan shouted. "It's our paper. You can't shut it down!"

"Oh yes, I can!" Dr. Carbles said. "And there's nothing you can do about it. Nobody will *ever* read this trash!"

Everybody was really upset. But Mrs. Lilly had a little smile on her face.

"I'm sorry to tell you this," she said quietly, "but people are *already* reading *The Ella Mentry Sentry.*"

"What?!" shouted Dr. Carbles as he waved the papers in the air. "How can anybody read it if I have all the pages?"

"Because they're reading the online edition," Mrs. Lilly told him. "*The Ella Mentry Sentry* is on the internet. I sent it to WikiLeaks. Thousands of people are probably reading it right now."

"Oh no!" shouted Mr. Klutz. "Everybody is going to think I have two wives, and that I don't wear underpants!"

"People are going to say I beat my wife!" shouted Mr. Docker.

"They'll say I'm a drunk!" shouted Miss Laney.

"And that I kill defenseless animals," shouted Mrs. Jafee.

Suddenly, there was a siren outside. I looked out the window. A police car pulled up to the school, and two cops got out. A minute later they were in our classroom.

"Which one of you is the principal of

this school?" one of the policemen asked.

"I am," said Mr. Klutz.

"Well, you're under arrest," said the policeman. "It's against the law to have more than one wife."

"But . . . but . . . but . . . this is all a big mistake, Officer," Mr. Klutz tried to explain. "I don't have—"

"You have the right to remain silent," interrupted the policeman as he got out a pair of handcuffs. "So be quiet. And pull up your pants."

The policeman handcuffed Mr. Klutz and led him away. The other policeman took a pad out of his pocket.

"Okay, we also need to arrest the guy

who beats his wife, the lady who burns down houses, the car thief, and, uh, who's the dog killer?" he asked.

"That would be me," said Mrs. Patty, raising her hand.

"The guy who kisses married women can stay," said the policeman, "and so can the illegal alien and the lady who thinks she sees Elvis in soup bowls. But we're

keeping an eye on you three."

He put handcuffs on Mr. Docker, Mrs. Yonkers, Ms. Coco, and Mrs. Patty. Then he led them out the doorway. It was cool! We got to see it live and in person.

Nobody said anything for a while after the police car drove away. Then Mrs. Lilly stood up and put her trench coat on.

"Well, my work is done here," she said. "You can thank me later. For now, I have to go."

"Do you have to go," I asked, "or do you have to *go*?"

"I mean, leave," said Mrs. Lilly.

"You don't need to use leaves," I told her. "There's toilet paper in the bathroom."

Dr. Carbles and just about all the other grown-ups left the classroom after that. The only one who was still there was Mr. Granite.

"Okay," said Mr. Granite, "maybe we can finally do our math lesson now. Turn to page twenty-three in your—"

He never got the chance to finish his sentence, because at that moment a loud bell rang.

Brrrrrrriiiiiinnnnnnnngggggg!

It was three o'clock! Time to go home! Yay! No math!

When I got home, my mom asked me what happened at school during the day.

"Nothing," I said.*

---

*Any time your parents ask what happened at school during the day, you should always say "Nothing." That's the first rule of being a kid.

Lies! All Lies!

I didn't know if school would be open on Monday, because Mr. Klutz and half the teachers were in jail. But when I got to school, the front door was open, and there were a bunch of substitute teachers in the halls.

Most of the kids were already in class when I got there. I put my stuff in my cubby and sat down.* And you'll never believe who walked into the door at that moment.

It was Mayor Hubble, who is like the king of the whole town! He walked right into the door!

"Ouch!" Mayor Hubble said. "That hurts!"

"Will you be our teacher today, Mayor?" asked Andrea, who never misses the chance to brownnose a grown-up.

"Yes," Mayor Hubble said, "we ran out of substitute teachers, so I'm filling in today."

---

*But not in my cubby. That would be weird.

"Is it true that you were going to the bathroom when a tree fell on your house?" Alexia asked the mayor.

"Yes, I was trapped in there for many hours."

"Well, at least you had a bathroom handy," I said.

The mayor opened up his briefcase and pulled out some papers. He passed one to each of us.

"The teachers were inspired by you

kids," Mayor Hubble said. "Over the week-end, they made a little newspaper just like yours. I thought you might want to look at it. There are some great human interest stories in here."

I looked at the newspaper. This is what the top headline said:

A.J. Picks Nose, Eats It!

"Ewwwwwwwww, disgusting!" Neil the nude kid shouted.

"Hey, A.J.," said Michael. "Did you really eat your nose?"

"No!" I shouted.

I wanted to go run away to Antarctica and live with the penguins. Then I looked at the other headlines on the page:

Michael Can't Tie His Own Shoes!

RYaN WiLL Eat ANYthiNg— EVeN Stuff that isN't Food!

UNDeR HiS CLOthes, NeiL IS Nude!

A.J. aNd ALexia: TWiNS sepaRated at BiRth!

ANdRea FaiLS SPeLLiNg Test!

Everybody was yelling and screaming and freaking out. And nobody was more upset than Andrea.

"That's a lie!" she shouted. "I never got less than an A plus on any test in my life!"

"The teachers can't print these lies about us!" shouted Neil the nude kid.

"Sure they can," said Mayor Hubble. "Did you ever hear of freedom of the press?"

"That's not fair!" we all shouted.

At that moment an announcement came

over the loudspeaker. We had to report to the all-purpose room for an assembly.

"It's time to go," said Mayor Hubble.

"Is it time to go," I asked, "or is it time to *go*?"

"It's time to go," said Mayor Hubble.

"What if we don't have to go?" asked Ryan.

"We *all* have to go," said Mayor Hubble.

"At the same time?" asked Michael.

"I don't have to go," I said.

"Me neither," said Alexia.

"I just went a few minutes ago," said Emily.

"I'll go later," said Neil the nude kid.

Well, that's pretty much what happened. Maybe the teachers will get out of jail soon. Maybe we'll publish another edition of *The Ella Mentry Sentry*. Maybe Mrs. Lilly will stop grabbing people's eyeballs. Maybe Tony Eagle will stop running into doors. Maybe they'll get that tree out of Mayor Hubble's bathroom. Maybe Andrea will explode. Maybe Mr. Klutz will stop pulling his pants down in school. Maybe we'll all get invited to one of Mrs. Yonkers's barbecues. Maybe Mr. Macky will stop kissing his wife in public. Maybe everybody will stop having to go all the time. Maybe we'll finally get through page twenty-three in our math books.

But it won't be easy!